Arctic Wolves

Heather Hammonds

Contents

Arctic Wolves

The **Arctic** is one of the coldest places on Earth.

Arctic wolves are found in the Arctic, on islands in Northern Canada. There are Arctic wolves in some parts of Greenland, too.

The Arctic is the area inside the Arctic Circle, around the North Pole.

Arctic wolves look different from other wolves, such as timber wolves.

Arctic wolves have a very thick white or pale-grey coat. Arctic wolves also have shorter ears and noses than timber wolves. They have lots of fur between the pads on their paws, too. These things help them to keep warm in the freezing Arctic weather.

The Arctic wolf's pale coat makes it hard to see in the snow.

The timber wolf has a darker coat than the Arctic wolf.

Arctic wolves live in family groups, just as other wolves do. These family groups are called "packs".

Wolf packs live, travel and hunt for food together. They run, play and eat on the cold, icy Arctic land, where not many animals can survive.

Arctic wolves are very powerful animals.
They are able to travel long distances
to hunt for musk oxen and caribou.
Musk oxen and caribou also live in the Arctic.

Arctic wolves hunt smaller animals such as Arctic hares, too.

Arctic wolves hunt Arctic hares for food.

Living in the Arctic

Arctic wolves live on an area of open, cold land called the Arctic **tundra**.

There are no trees on the tundra.

Small grasses and other plants grow on the hard rocks and ground.

The sun shines all day and night during the summer months.

In the coldest winter months, it is dark all day and night.

It is so cold in the Arctic tundra that the ground just under the surface stays frozen all year round! This frozen ground is called "permafrost".

Even in summer, the Arctic tundra is a very cold place.

Some animals and birds, such as snow geese, spend part of the year in the Arctic and travel south to warmer places for winter.

Arctic wolves, as well as some other animals such as **polar** bears and musk oxen, live in the Arctic all year round.

The wolves continue to hunt for food during the coldest parts of winter.

Snow geese fly south away from the Arctic for the winter.

Arctic wolves stay in the Arctic in all seasons.

Wolf Packs

Family Life

Arctic wolf packs are usually made up of several members of one family. The **dominant**, or leading, male and female in the pack are the parents of the other wolves.

At around two or three years of age, young wolves may leave the pack. They will find a mate and start a new pack.

Adult wolves in an Arctic wolf pack lead the younger wolves.

Arctic wolves communicate with each other by sniffing, whimpering, growling and howling. They also use their bodies to show what they are feeling.

an Arctic wolf howling

A more dominant wolf may stand over another wolf and growl.
The less dominant wolf may lie down or tuck its tail between its legs when this happens.

Arctic wolves can communicate by leaving smells around to mark out the places where they live.

This older wolf is growling at a younger wolf.

Hunting for Food

When Arctic wolves hunt for food, they work as a team. By working together, the wolves can catch the larger animals they eat, such as musk oxen. One large musk ox can feed many wolves!

The wolves travel around their **territory**, searching for musk oxen, caribou and other animals.

This pack of Arctic wolves is hunting a group of large musk oxen.

Arctic wolves will try to find an animal that is easier to catch in a herd of musk oxen or caribou.
This may be an old or sick animal, or a very young animal.
The adult wolves in the pack will then work together to separate the weaker animal from the herd.

An Arctic wolf pack works together to find food.

Arctic wolves sometimes go without food for many days while looking for their next meal.

Arctic Wolf Puppies

Newborn Puppies

Arctic wolf puppies are born in the spring. A mother wolf gives birth to her **litter** of puppies in a small den.

The puppies are very small and cannot see or hear when they are first born. They drink their mother's milk.

Arctic wolf puppies are born in a small den.

Arctic wolf puppies have darker fur when they are young.

Arctic wolves must choose a small cave or a shelter under rocks for a den. The ground in the Arctic is too hard for them to dig a den themselves.

Arctic wolf puppies' eyes open when they are 11 to 15 days old. Their ears open a little later, but by 21 days they can hear, too.

From around four weeks of age, the puppies begin to eat meat. Older wolves in the pack help bring food for the puppies to eat. The older wolves regurgitate, or bring up, food from their stomach for the puppies.

This Arctic wolf puppy is about to eat meat from the mouth of an adult wolf.

Growing Up

As Arctic wolf puppies grow older, they leave their den. The other members of the wolf pack continue to bring them food.

Arctic wolf puppies are very playful. They learn how to behave around other wolves by playing with each other, and with other wolves in the pack.

These Arctic wolf puppies are learning how to behave by playing.

When Arctic wolf puppies grow bigger, they begin to go on hunting trips with the older wolves. The puppies learn how to travel across the Arctic tundra safely. They watch the older wolves hunt, and they learn about hunting.

Young wolf puppies must learn how to hunt from the older wolves.

Arctic Wolves and Humans

Arctic wolves have very little contact with humans. This is because the wolves live in one of the most **remote** places on Earth. Fewer people live in the Arctic than in warmer places on Earth.

Some people live on Ellesmere Island, Canada, where Arctic wolves also live.

The **Inuit peoples** (say: *In-yoo-it*) of the Arctic tell stories about a huge wolf, called an Amarok.

Today, scientists travel to the Arctic to study Arctic wolves. They learn how the wolves survive in the cold Arctic climate, and how the members of a wolf pack live together.

Many Arctic wolves are not afraid of people,
as they have not seen them before.
They will allow scientists to follow them about
and get close to them.

A scientist takes a photo of an Arctic wolf on Ellesmere Island.

Threats to Arctic Wolves

Arctic wolves face very few threats from other animals. They are one of the **apex predators** in the Arctic, along with polar bears.

However, Arctic weather is a threat to young Arctic wolves during their first winter. It is very cold, and sometimes there is not enough food.

Arctic wolves sometimes find it hard to get enough food in the harsh Arctic winter.

Arctic wolves can also be a threat to each other.
Wolf packs are not friendly to other wolves
that enter their territory.
They may fight with a wolf who is alone
and hunting for food or looking for a mate.
They may try to harm it or chase it away.

Arctic wolves protect their own territory.

Arctic wolves also face the threat of **climate change**.

Grasses and other plants in the Arctic have **adapted** to today's Arctic climate. However, they may not grow as well, or survive at all, as the climate changes.

Musk oxen, caribou and Arctic hares eat Arctic plants. When there is less food for them, many do not survive.

Without as many musk oxen and other Arctic animals to hunt, Arctic wolves also go hungry. Some wolves do not survive, as there is not enough food to go around.

When there are fewer animals around to hunt for food, Arctic wolves may not survive.

Scientists know the Arctic is warming much faster than other places on Earth.

Arctic wolves are special members of the wolf family.
They are able to survive in one of the coldest places on Earth!

Arctic wolves have an important place
in the Arctic environment.
They must be protected, along with the other animals
and plants that live there.

Glossary

adapted (*verb*) become used to something, such as weather or climate

apex predators (*noun*) the top hunters among the animals in an area

Arctic (*proper noun*) the area around the North Pole, including sea, ice and land

climate change (*noun*) a change in weather patterns around the world

dominant (*adjective*) in charge, or the boss over others

Inuit peoples (*proper noun*) Indigenous peoples of Canada, Alaska and Greenland

litter (*noun*) a group of animal babies of the same age, from the same mother

polar (*adjective*) to do with the North or South Poles – the northernmost and southernmost points of Earth

remote (*adjective*) far away from other people and towns

territory (*noun*) an area of land where a wolf pack lives and hunts

tundra (*noun*) a very cold area with hard, frozen ground where trees do not grow

Index